W9-BWD-617

TINY
THE SNOW DOG

TINY

by Cari Meister
illustrated by Rich Davis

PUFFIN BOOKS

PUFFIN BOOKS
Published by the Penguin Group
Penguin Putnam Books for Young Readers,
345 Hudson Street, New York, New York 10014, U.S.A.
Penguin Books Ltd, 27 Wrights Lane, London W8 5TZ, England
Penguin Books Australia Ltd, Ringwood, Victoria, Australia
Penguin Books Canada Ltd, 10 Alcorn Avenue, Toronto, Ontario, Canada M4V 3B2
Penguin Books (N.Z.) Ltd, 182-190 Wairau Road, Auckland 10, New Zealand

Penguin Books Ltd, Registered Offices: Harmondsworth, Middlesex, England

First published in the United States of America simultaneously by Viking and Puffin
Books, divisions of Penguin Putnam Books for Young Readers, 2001

10 9 8 7 6

Text copyright © Cari Meister, 2001
Illustrations copyright © Rich Davis, 2001

LIBRARY OF CONGRESS CATALOGING-IN-PUBLICATION DATA
Meister, Cari
Tiny the snow dog / Cari Meister ; illustrated by Rich Davis.
    p.   cm. — (Viking easy-to-read)
Summary: Tiny and his owner play in the snow and Tiny becomes a snow dog.
ISBN 0-670-89117-7 (hc.)—ISBN 0-14-056708-9 (pbk.)
[1. Snow—Fiction. 2. Dogs—Fiction.] I. Davis, Rich, date. II. Title. III. Series.
PZ7.M515916 Th 2001 [E]—dc21 99-088385

Puffin Easy-to-Read ISBN 0-14-056708-9
Puffin® and Easy-to-Read® are registered trademarks of Penguin Putnam Inc.

Printed in Hong Kong

Reading Level 1.4

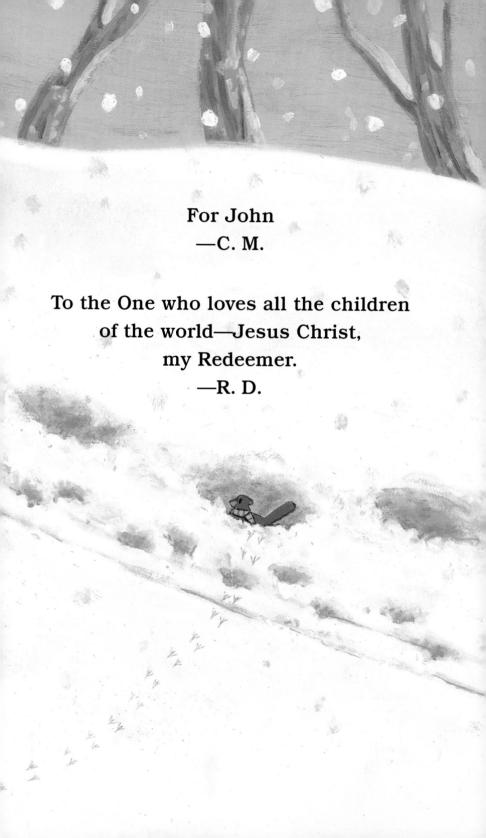

For John
—C. M.

To the One who loves all the children
of the world—Jesus Christ,
my Redeemer.
—R. D.

This is Tiny.

He is my dog.

Tiny loves winter.

I do, too.

Look, Tiny! Snow!

Tiny wants to go out. I do, too.

Brrr! It is cold.
We need warm hats.

Tiny has a new hat.

I do, too.

Ready? Go!

I toss a snowball. Tiny runs.

Tiny runs and runs.

Oh no! Where is Tiny?

I do not see him.

I look by the barn.

No Tiny.

I look by the hill.

No Tiny.

I look and look and look.

Still no Tiny.

Tiny, where are you?

Crunch, crunch, crunch.

What is that?

Crunch, crunch, crunch.

A snow monster.
A snow monster is coming to get me!

Slurp!

It is Tiny! Tiny is the snow monster.

Come on, Tiny.

Time to go home.

Good snow dog.